THE WATER MARGIN

SHI NAI

REAL READS

www.realreads.co.uk

Retold by Chi
Illustrated by S

D1580698

Published by Real Reads Ltd
Stroud, Gloucestershire, UK
www.realreads.co.uk

First published in 2011

ISBN 978-1-906230-37-1

Printed in Singapore by Imago Ltd
Designed by Lucy Guenot
Typeset by Bookcraft Ltd, Stroud, Gloucestershire

CONTENTS

THE CHARACTERS

'Monk' Lu Zhishen and 'Leopard' Lin Chong

Lu and Lin are two of the first fugitives to join the outlaws at Mount Liang. What makes them become outlaws in the first place?

'King' Chao Gai and 'Resourceful' Wu Yong

Chao is the original leader of the outlaws at Mount Liang. Wu is his strategist. Between them they devise schemes to rob the rich and help the poor.

'Welcome Rain' Song Jiang

Song admires the outlaws at Mount Liang but is determined to remain loyal to his country. Will he change his mind and join them?

'Pilgrim' Wu Song and 'Whirlwind' Li Kui

Wu and Li are known for their great strength. Will their heroic acts win the respect of the outlaws at Mount Liang?

'Daredevil' Shi Xiu and 'Sickman' Yang Xiong

Shi and Yang have vowed to treat each other as brothers. Can their friendship stand the tests of suspicion and betrayal?

'Unicorn' Lu Junyi and 'Dragon' Gongsun Sheng

Lu and Gongsun are both reluctant to join the outlaws at Mount Liang. What makes them change their minds?

'Clubs' Huyan Zhuo and 'Blade' Guan Sheng

Huyan and Guan lead the imperial troops in their assaults on Mount Liang. Can they successfully defeat the outlaws?

5

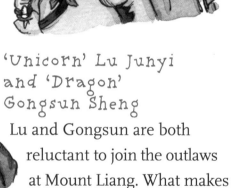

Lu Zhishen, 'Monk'
魯智深

Lin Chong, 'Leopard'
林冲

LEADER OF THE LIANG OUTLAWS

Chao Gai 'King'
晁蓋

THE WATER

The marshes of Mount Liang

The main characters in the story have their names in orange

Wu Yong 'Resourceful'
吳用

Song Jiang 'Welcome Rain'
宋江

Wu Song 'Pilgrim'
武松

Li Kui 'Whirlwind'
李逵

Suo Chao 'Charge Ahead'
索超

Yan Qing 'Stealthy Wanderer'
燕青

Lu Junyi 'Unicorn'
盧俊義

Gongsun Sheng 'Dragon'
公孫勝

Huyan Zhou 'Clubs'
呼延灼

Guan Sheng 'Blade'
關勝

Dai Zong 'Magic Traveller'
戴宗

Chai Jin 'Little Whirlwind'
柴進

Dong Ping 'Double Spears'
董平

Liu Tang 'Red-haired Devil'
劉唐

Mu Hong 'Unrestrained'
慕弘

Zhang Heng 'Boatman'
張橫

Zhang Shun 'Waveman'
張順

MARGIN

Li Jun 'River Dragon' 李俊

Li Ying 'Attacking Hawk' 李應

Qin Ming 'Thunderbolt' 秦明

THE 36 'HEAVENLY SPIRITS'

史進 Shi Jin 'Dragon Tattoos'

Ruan Xiaoqi 'Ruler of Hell' 阮小七

阮小二 Ruan Xiaoer 'Unmoveable'

Ruan Xiaowu 'Deadly Smile'

阮小五

石秀 Shi Xiu 'Daredevil'

楊雄 Yang Xiong 'Sickman'

花榮 Hua Rong 'Little General'

雷橫 Lei Heng 'Winged Tiger'

Zhu Tong 'Beautiful Beard' 朱仝

Xu Ning 'Golden Lance' 徐寧

Xie Zhen 'Two-headed Serpent' 解寶

楊志

解珍

Xie Bao 'Scorpion'

Yang Zhi 'Blue-faced Beast'

張清

THE 72 'EARTHLY DEMONS'

Zhang Qing 'Featherless Arrow'

THE WATER MARGIN

For many decades the Song Empire had been prosperous and strong. It was well served by humble emperors and their diligent servants, and the people lived in peace and happiness.

Then, without any warning, a terrible plague broke out. It spread to every corner of the empire. The emperor, concerned for his people, decided to appoint a renowned spiritual master to lead the empire in praying for heavenly blessings. Marshal Hong was sent to meet the guru at his temple and bring him back to the capital.

Marshal Hong was an arrogant man. When he reached the temple where the guru lived, he insisted on being given a tour. There was one room whose door was tightly locked. Ignoring the temple official's advice, Hong ordered that the door be opened. Inside the room was nothing but a stone tablet covering a large hole in the ground. Four words were engraved into the tablet – 'Thus revealed with Hong.'

Assuming the words referred to him, Hong ordered that the tablet be removed.

Boom!

A mass of smoke blasted out of the hole and up into the sky, destroying half of the temple roof. As Marshal Hong and the temple official ducked for cover, the smoke transformed into a hundred and eight beams of golden light, which radiated in all directions and then disappeared.

Trembling, Hong demanded to know what had happened. With a sour face the temple official explained. 'Deep in that hole were thirty-six heavenly spirits and seventy-two earthly demons imprisoned by the spiritual master. Now that you have let them out the whole world will be devastated.'

Marshal Hong was deeply ashamed. When he returned to the capital he did not tell the emperor what he had done. As we shall see, however, the results of Hong's arrogance would have enormous consequences in the years to come. The one hundred and eight spirits released by Hong would return as mortal heroes, and in time would change the course of the Song Empire.

The plague eventually passed, and the empire recovered. Some sixty years later a handsome clown named Gao Qiu arrived at the capital. Capable of many circus tricks, Gao knew exactly how to please his audience, especially the emperor of the time. The emperor was so delighted by Gao's excellent juggling that the clown was awarded with a high-ranking post in the government.

Power went to Gao's head. He thought he was now ringmaster of the whole circus. He bullied the other officials and sacked many of those most loyal to the emperor. In their place Gao promoted his own friends and relatives to high power.

At the same time as Gao was building his empire-within-an-empire, several other people who would play an important part in our story were involved in struggles of their own.

Lu Zhishen was a soldier. He was large and strong, with a very short temper that often caused him a great deal of trouble.

One day he was drinking at a local inn and heard a woman crying in the next room. When Lu asked her what was wrong, the woman explained, 'The landowner wants me to marry him, or he will take away my family's land!'

Lu went straight to the landowner and demanded justice. He was so angry that he punched the landowner repeatedly, and ended up killing him. Lu panicked. Desperate to evade the police, he shaved his head and disguised himself as a monk in a local Buddhist temple.

But 'Monk' Lu found the disguise very hard. He continued eating meat and drinking

wine, which were forbidden by Buddhist rules. Under the influence of alcohol, he insulted his master and attacked those temple officials who tried to discipline him. One day, completely drunk, he thought the Buddha's statue was mocking him and smashed it into pieces.

Lu realised that he had gone too far. He was very upset with himself, and left the temple.

Lin Chong was the senior military instructor of eight hundred thousand imperial troops. He was sturdy and tall, with a big head and fierce eyes like those of a wild cat, which is why many people called him 'Leopard' Lin. Lin loved his beautiful wife very much.

One day the provincial governor, who was the nephew of Gao, the emperor's favourite clown, saw Lin's beautiful wife in the market. 'She is so beautiful that I want her as a concubine!' he said to himself. He decided that the best way to get Lin out of the way and steal his wife was to accuse him of being disrespectful to government officials. He had Lin thrown into jail.

Lin had little chance against the combined power of the governor and Gao, his high-placed uncle. He was sentenced to exile in a distant land. The governor bribed the two guards escorting Lin to kill him along the way. The guards forced Lin to wash his feet in boiling water, then made him walk in heavy shackles with his blistered feet. They reached some thick woods, and the guards thought it was now a good time to kill Lin. They tied him to a tree and pulled out their knives.

'Halt!' a voice boomed out behind them.

The guards turned in surprise to see Lu Zhishen, still dressed as a monk, his face distorted with anger as he saw the brutality being meted out to a defenceless man. They dropped their knives and cowered. Lin was untied and unshackled, thanking Lu profusely for saving his life.

Remembering that the guards were only following the governor's orders, Lin begged Lu to spare their lives. The grateful guards ran off through the woods.

Like many people at that time who were concerned about corruption in the imperial court, Lin and Lu had heard many stories about the 'righteous bandits', outlaws who lived in the sparsely-inhabited marshlands of nearby Mount Liang. There were many stories about the Mount Liang outlaws confiscating valuables from rich people who were selfish and corrupt, and using the money to help the poor.

The leader of the outlaws, 'King' Chao Gai, had once been a rich man and a law-abiding citizen. Chao, together with his strategist, 'Resourceful' Wu Yong, were disgusted by a local official who kept sending valuable gifts to the capital as a bribe to Gao, the emperor's favourite clown. They had led a group of followers to confiscate the gifts, sell them, and distribute the money to help those in poverty.

Determined to continue their fight against the corrupt government, Chao and Wu and their followers had settled in the Mount Liang marshlands, gradually winning the hearts of the locals. Now that they were both fugitives too, Lin and Lu decided to travel to Mount Liang, and when Chao heard about their arrival he gladly took them in and treated them as brothers.

Song Jiang was a provincial clerk who loved to help other people, which had earned him the nickname 'Welcome Rain'. After Chao and Wu and their supporters had robbed the corrupt local official of the bribes destined for Gao's treasury, Song was ordered by his superiors to attack and capture the Mount Liang outlaws.

Song secretly admired the Mount Liang outlaws as true heroes of the people, so he deliberately postponed dealing with the order. He also had a good excuse not to deal with it straight away – he had very recently married a local girl.

What Song did not know was that his wife had only married him for his money. Soon she was having an affair with another man, and threatened that she would expose Song as a supporter of the outlaws. When Song discovered her plans he was so angry that he killed her. He was arrested by the police and thrown into jail.

While Song suffered in jail, more and more rebels were on their way to join the righteous outlaws in the Mount Liang marshes. One of them was Wu Song, a large man with a fearsome temper who was a brilliant fighter with his long staff.

Wu stopped at an inn to have a drink. The inn brewed a liquor which was so famously strong that the innkeeper refused to allow anyone more than three bowlfuls. Wu wasn't having any of it, and insisted on ordering more.

'You'll regret it,' said the innkeeper, 'especially as you'll need all your wits about you to steer clear of the man-eating tiger that lives on the hill you're about to climb.'

Wu ignored the innkeeper, and didn't stop drinking until he had eighteen bowls of liquor inside him.

'You're just trying to keep me here to buy more of your liquor,' Wu burped. 'Besides, who's afraid of a cat?'

Wu climbed the hill and entered a forest. Suddenly, with an almighty roar, a huge tiger jumped out of the trees, ready to attack. Wu quickly pulled out his staff. As the tiger rushed towards him he stepped aside to let it pass, striking the tiger so hard on its back that the staff broke in two.

The tiger, more furious than ever, roared in pain. It turned round and bared its teeth. It jumped, but Wu was ready. Throwing away the stump of his staff, Wu stepped back. The tiger landed with a thud right in front of him. He grabbed its ears and, using all his strength, pressed its head hard into the ground.

The liquor burned inside Wu as he fought. Clutching the tiger's head with his left hand, he raised his right fist and hit the beast again and again. After sixty or seventy blows, the tiger finally stopped struggling. It lay motionless, blood streaming from its head.

Wu dragged the dead tiger down the hill to the nearest town, and soon became the local hero, a great warrior who rid the town of its feared predator.

But Wu now had other concerns on his mind. His brother had recently been married to a beautiful woman named Lotus, and Wu was keen to go home and visit them. When Wu arrived he was shocked to find his brother was dead. The neighbours told the grief-stricken Wu that Lotus had been having an affair, and when the body was examined by the coroner it was revealed that Wu's brother had been stabbed and then poisoned.

Wu interrogated Lotus and her lover, who eventually admitted that they had indeed murdered his brother. Wu flew into a rage and took matters into his own hands. He grabbed a sabre and swung it at Lotus, taking off her head with one blow. Then he went to find her lover and killed him too.

Knowing that he had done wrong, Wu went to the police to confess to the double killing. Although the judge understood why Wu had done such a dreadful thing, and saw that there was some justice in it, he had no choice other than to sentence him to exile in the distant province of Mengzhou.

Wu's sense of justice and his reputation as a tiger-killing hero travelled ahead of him. While he was in exile he befriended a group of outlaws who honoured him as their leader. Together they decided to travel to Mount Liang and join the outlaws. To conceal his true identity, Wu dressed in the robes of a Taoist priest and gained the nickname 'Pilgrim'.

Wu and his men rescued 'Welcome Rain' Song from the prison where he had been languishing. Despite his desire for freedom and his friendship with Wu, however, Song refused to become a bandit, even a righteous one.

'I was raised to love my father and respect his wishes,' Song said to Wu, 'and my father taught me to be loyal to my country. Do you want me to betray both my father and my country?'

Wu said goodbye to Song, and led his men back to Mount Liang. Song returned to prison to serve his sentence, but he was accused of cooperating with the outlaws in his escape, and

sentenced to death. The news soon reached Mount Liang, where the outlaws had long admired Song for his heroic act of delaying the government's attack on them. Everyone was determined to do their best to rescue 'Welcome Rain' Song.

On the day Song was to be executed, the Mount Liang rebels attacked the government building in force. They fought brilliantly, using bows and arrows, sabres, swords, spears, staffs and slingshots. The executioner raised his axe over Song's head, but just as he was to bring it down a hail of daggers thrown by the outlaws soared through the air and felled him to the ground. The crowd screamed and ran for their lives.

Suddenly a dark-skinned man jumped out of the crowd. Waving two gigantic axes, he fought off the guards and slashed the ropes that bound Song's hands and feet. He pulled Song onto his back and dashed into a nearby ally, calling the outlaws to follow him.

'Retreat!' he yelled. 'The provincial army is coming!'

The outlaws followed the dark-skinned man through the narrow streets, turning this way and that until they had finally lost the pursuing army. It was only then that they all stopped to thank the man, whose name turned out to be Li Kui. They nicknamed him 'Whirlwind' because he fought with such strength and speed.

The outlaws brought Song back to Mount Liang, where he thanked them profusely. Having so narrowly escaped death, he had finally lost faith in the corrupt government and decided to join the outlaws.

By now there were nearly a thousand outlaws living in the marshes of Mount Liang. They worked together to construct fortresses, dig trenches, and set up guard posts along the rivers and swamps. As many of them used to be farmers, fishermen, carpenters and plumbers, they grew their own rice, vegetables and livestock, and built a series of living quarters. They even produced their own weapons, using all kinds of timber, metals and stone found in the mountains. Under the training of experienced warriors like Lu, Lin, Wu and Li, they perfected their fighting skills.

Meanwhile two sworn brothers named Yang Xiong and Shi Xiu were sitting and talking at a nearby inn. Yang worked in the prison as an executioner, and was nicknamed 'Sickman' because of his pale skin. Shi, a butcher, was nicknamed 'Daredevil' because of his stubbornness in maintaining what he considered to be justice.

Yang had recently married a beautiful woman named Qiaoyun, but Shi had discovered that Qiaoyun was having an affair with a monk from the local monastery. When he told Yang, the young man punched his fist on the table. 'I'll divorce her as soon as I get home!' he shouted.

'No,' said Shi. 'You cannot be sure that what I say is true. You must pretend that you have heard nothing, and wait until you catch them together. Then you'll have definite proof.'

Yang agreed with Shi, but he was so upset that he could not stop drinking, as if the liquor might be able to smother the blazing fury in his heart.

When Yang got home that night, he was completely drunk. As Qiaoyun helped him into bed, he mumbled angrily, 'You ... and a monk ... You just wait ... '

When Qiaoyun realised that her husband knew about the affair, she hatched a plan. The next morning, when Yang woke up, he was surprised to see his wife crying.

'What is it, Qiaoyun?' he asked.

'It's your best friend and sworn brother Shi,' wailed Qiaoyun through her tears. 'He tried to force himself upon me, saying he loved me. He is a dishonourable man! You must stop being friends with that wretched Shi.'

'How can this be!' shouted Yang. Later that day he told Shi that they could no longer be sworn brothers.

Shi knew that he had to prove his innocence in order to win back Yang's friendship. The next morning the monk was found dead. At first only Shi knew that the monk had died at his hand, but once the monk was dead rumours began to spread around the neighbourhood that he had been killed because of an affair he had been having with the executioner's wife. When Yang heard the rumours he realised that Shi had been telling the truth, and that Qiaoyun had been lying.

Yang sought out Shi and apologised profusely. Together they questioned Qiaoyun until she confessed. Yang was furious and lost his temper; before he knew what he was doing Qiaoyun, his deceitful wife, lay dead.

Yang and Shi needed to leave before the law caught up with them. The obvious choice was for them to go and join the 'righteous outlaws' in the marshlands of Mount Liang.

Soon after Yang and Shi arrived at Mount
Liang, they heard that the outlaws were
about to be attacked by imperial government
troops. Seeing a chance to further expand his
influence in the imperial court, the clown
Gao Qiu had persuaded the emperor that the
outlaws were now strong enough to warrant
an imperial army assault on their mountain
stronghold. Gao also sent his own brother, Gao
Lian, to command the troops.

'Leopard' Lin led the outlaws in an
attempt to ambush the imperial army's initial
attack.

Just as Lin thought his men were forceful
enough to defeat the troops, Gao, at the head
of the imperial ranks, suddenly wielded his
sword and looked up at the sky. 'Blow!' he
commanded.

The sky above Mount Liang darkened.

A fierce wind began to blow, snapping tree branches and flagpoles and raising a great sandstorm which blinded Lin's men and their horses. Many of them were killed or captured by the imperial troops, forcing Lin to retreat.

This was the first defeat the outlaws had ever experienced. However, 'Resourceful' Wu knew how to offset such dark magic. He taught 'Welcome Rain' Song some of his most powerful magical chants and asked Song to organise a counter-attack.

When Gao again called for the wind to blow, Song pulled out his own sword and recited Wu's chants. The strong winds turned, driving the sandstorm back towards the panicking imperial troops.

But Gao had more magic to call upon. Brandishing his sword, he dispersed the wind and used his powers to create a horde of small biting animals and poisonous insects. Song's men had to retreat in haste, but many of them were bitten or stung by the bizarre creatures.

'I know only one man who can counter such dark magic,' Wu told the outlaws as they gathered to work out what to do. 'His name is Gongsun Sheng, a wise guru who lives nearby on the other side of the mountain. He is so wise that many call him "Dragon".' To show their sincerity in requesting the guru's assistance, Wu decided to act as representative of the outlaws and pay Gongsun a visit. 'Whirlwind' Li volunteered to accompany Wu.

When Wu and Li arrived at Gongsun's dwelling, the only person they saw was an old woman who claimed to be the guru's mother. Wu asked politely to see Gongsun, but she refused to let them in. No matter how much Wu begged and explained the urgency of their visit, she only shook her head.

Li was now becoming very impatient. He took his axes from his belt and stepped forward. 'Come out, Gongsun, wherever you are!' he shouted. 'If you don't I'll kill your precious mother!' Li raised his axes above the old woman's head.

Suddenly a man ran out of the house. With a wave of his hand he sent Li's axes soaring into the sky. 'How dare you threaten my dear mother like that!' Gongsun yelled at Li and Wu.

Wu apologised profusely on behalf of Li, who had slipped away in shame to look for his axes. Wu explained the danger faced by the Mount Liang outlaws and begged Gongsun to help them.

The guru shook his head. 'A man of spiritual practice should not get involved in earthly struggles,' he said. 'More importantly, I need to look after my frail mother.'

'Please Gongsun,' pleaded Wu, 'with all your wisdom and magical power please help us!' Gongsun again shook his head, and started to help his mother back into the house.

Just at that moment Li returned with his axes. He fell to his knees and held his axes close to his own neck. 'I'm deeply sorry for being rude to your mother,' he said quietly. 'I'm willing to kill myself as a punishment if only you can save my fellows at Mount Liang!' Li banged his forehead on the ground to show his remorse. Blood and tears soon began to stream down his face.

The old woman spoke. 'My son,' she said to Gongsun, 'this is a good man. You had better go and help his friends.' Gongsun reluctantly obeyed his mother's order.

As soon as 'Dragon' Gongsun arrived at Mount Liang he led the outlaws in a fierce battle against Gao's imperial troops. Again Gao waved his sword and created a horde of biting animals and insects.

As soon as he saw what Gao had created, Gongsun pointed two of his fingers at the weird creatures. 'Away!' he shouted, and from his fingers shot a beam of golden light that transformed into hundreds of golden arrows which pierced every one of Gao's creatures. It was only then that the rebels could see that the bizarre creatures were only shapes of animals and insects cut out of paper.

Seeing his dark magic so easily rebuffed, Gao waved his sword again and shouted 'Rise!' A dark cloud appeared under his feet and carried him into the air, but Gongsun had already seen this coming.

Pointing his fingers at the cloud, Gongsun shouted 'Fall!' Immediately the dark cloud was dispersed and Gao fell heavily to the ground.

'Whirlwind' Li was waiting for him with his sharpened axes, and severed Gao's head from his body with one stroke.

Having lost their commander and witnessed the brilliant fighting power demonstrated by the Mount Liang outlaws, many of the imperial troops dropped their weapons and surrendered. The rest ran for their lives.

When he heard that his brother had been killed by the outlaws, Gao Qiu vowed to destroy them once and for all. He persuaded the emperor that the only course of action was to send five thousand imperial troops to demolish all the 'thieves and thugs' of Mount Liang. 'The empire will be in grave danger if even one of these looters and rioters is spared,' Gao explained.

The commander of the new imperial force was Huyan Zhuo, a brave army officer whose weapons were two steel clubs. To ensure that 'Clubs' Huyan and the imperial army would be victorious, Gao talked the emperor into providing Huyan's troops with the best horses, armour, weapons and provisions the government could afford.

'Kill them all,' Gao told Huyan, 'or don't come back!'

As soon as the imperial troops received their orders, the Mount Liang outlaws were informed of the forthcoming battle. Wu warned everyone that Huyan was a great military leader whose wisdom and fighting skills should not be underestimated.

Three days later, Song led the best of Mount Liang's warriors to confront the imperial troops. As Lin and Lu took turns to fight Huyan, Yang and Shi ordered their men to assault the troops from the left while another group of outlaws, commanded by Wu and Li, ambushed them from the right.

As soon as there was a chance for Lin and Lu to draw back, thus encouraging the imperial troops to advance, Song brought his men forward to launch a mighty frontal attack while the others cut off their retreat. Once the troops were surrounded they could only surrender or be destroyed.

That was the rebels' plan, but even when the imperial troops were completely surrounded Huyan was confident that his forces could prevail. His secret weapon was to chain his horses together and shield them and their riders with heavy steel armour. The sound of them moving forward was like thunder, a massive mobile fortress that was strong enough to crash through the outlaws' defences and destroy them underfoot.

Seeing that they could not survive such an attack, Song ordered his men to retreat. They needed a new plan.

Huyan divided his imperial troops into a hundred groups, each of which consisted of thirty men on horses. Each group's horses were chained together, so they moved forward like a wall of steel, destroying whoever dared to confront it. Huyan ordered his remaining two thousand troops to stay behind and only attack when the outlaws appeared to be retreating.

Again Song led his men out for a battle, but again defeat was inevitable. Huyan's heavy armour spread out over the hills and plains around the marshes, overcoming the outlaws with ease. Song lost many men and horses that day, and those that could escaped by the boats which had been moored in the marshy waterways in case retreat became the only choice.

The outlaws had not yet run out of ideas, however, and 'Resourceful' Wu came up with a plan. Wu had studied closely how Huyan's troops attacked, and realised that the chained horses had one very specific weakness. Wu designed a special weapon like a spear with a steel hook on the end, and trained a hundred of his men exactly how to use it.

The next day, when Huyan ordered the imperial troops to attack, Wu sent his hundred trained men in groups of ten to taunt Huyan's chained horsemen. Huyan's men saw them as easy targets, and rode after them. The rebel groups ran into nearby scrub and bushes, shouting and jeering at the imperial troops. As soon as Huyan's horsemen entered the bushes, the outlaws hiding there used their weapons to hook the horses' legs and trip them up. As the horses were chained together they crashed like dominos, tumbling their armoured riders to the ground. In less than two hours nearly all of Huyan's troops were either captured or killed by the outlaws.

Having lost the battle and all his horses, men and weapons, Huyan knew he could never report back to Gao Qiu. He took the only possible course of action which would save his life; he surrendered and became one of the Mount Liang outlaws.

The outlaws celebrated their victory over the imperial troops, but very soon afterwards they heard that their leader, 'King' Chao, had been killed by a poisoned arrow in a fierce battle against the nearby city of Daming. Chao had been a strong leader, protecting the outlaws and making sure that they were always well organised, so his loss was felt deeply.

Everyone agreed that Song should lead the outlaws in their struggle against corruption and injustice. Song agreed, but insisted that whoever was able to avenge the death of Chao should eventually become the new leader of the Mount Liang outlaws.

In order to enhance the fighting skills of the outlaws, Song decided to enlist the help of Lu Junyi, the greatest warrior in Daming. Lu's nickname was 'Unicorn' because he fought with a long stick.

'Sickman' Yang and 'Daredevil' Shi were sent to capture Lu. Though Lu was a better warrior than the two of them combined, they forced him to retreat towards a nearby river, where several of the outlaws had dressed up as local fishermen with a boat. Desperate to escape Yang and Shi, Lu boarded the boat and demanded to be taken across the river. He was immediately seized by the outlaws and brought back to Mount Liang.

Lu refused to join the outlaws no matter how politely they asked, so they reluctantly let him go. However, there were already widespread rumours that he had become one of the bandits living on Mount Liang. Even worse, in his absence Lu's wife had found herself a new lover. When Lu returned home his wife immediately informed the police, so Lu was arrested, thrown into Daming jail, and sentenced to death.

When they heard what had happened, Song and the outlaws sent a letter to the governor of Daming. 'If you hurt so much as a single hair on Lu's head,' the letter said, 'we will destroy you and all your officials.'

The governor knew that these were no idle threats. He urgently sought help from Gao Qiu, who had now taken over what little power the emperor still possessed and was even more determined to destroy the Mount Liang outlaws. A new army official named Guan Sheng, called 'Blade' after his favourite green crescent scimitar, was appointed to command the imperial troops.

'Blade' Guan warned that the outlaws would launch their attack on Daming very soon. Rather than confronting the outlaws there, he decided to march straight to Mount Liang and attack the rebels' headquarters. It was a smart plan, but Wu had already seen it coming and was ready with a plan of his own.

Wu's secret weapon was Huyan, who met Guan as the imperial army arrived in force at Mount Liang. Guan knew all about Huyan's exploits against the outlaws, so it wasn't hard for Huyan to convince Guan that they were really both on the same side.

The tale that Huyan told Guan was that both he and Song were loyal government servants who had been forced to join the outlaws. Now that Guan had arrived with his imperial troops, Huyan and Song would do all they could to help them destroy the outlaws.

The next day Huyan fought heroically on the imperial front line against Song's men, winning the admiration of Guan and his troops. When the day's fighting ended Huyan told Guan that Song's men intended to surrender that very night in a nearby valley.

Guan led his troops to the valley, all ready to take the outlaw forces captive. It was only when they were surrounded by heavily armed outlaws that Guan realised it was a trap. Guan and his men surrendered, boosting the numbers at Mount Liang to nearly ten thousand.

Now it was time for the outlaws to rescue Lu from Daming Prison.

It was Chinese New Year, and the city was busy organising the annual lantern festival. Streets and public buildings were decorated with colourful lanterns, and there were to be parades and fireworks, singers and dancers.

Half of the outlaws disguised themselves as beggars, monks, street performers and visitors. They arrived in the evening and mingled with the crowds around the government building, which held the most spectacular lantern display in the city.

The remaining outlaws, led by Song, rode their horses towards the city gate. As they arrived, Song launched a rocket into the night sky, signalling that it was time for action. The outlaws already in the city set fires at the corners of the government building. The crowd screamed and panicked, running for their lives, and while the guards and officials

were busy dealing with the chaos the outlaws broke into the prison to rescue Lu.

Other outlaws overcame the guards defending the city gate and opened it wide, letting in Song and his horsemen. The combined outlaw force fought heroically until every last official and guard had been driven from Daming.

Song now ordered his men to put out the fires and comfort those who had suffered loss and damage. The city treasury and warehouse were unlocked so that government money and provisions could be distributed to all who needed them. The outlaws then left quietly, taking nothing with them but Lu.

To thank the outlaws for saving his life, Lu agreed to join their fight against the corrupt imperial government. By now there were one hundred and eight heroes commanding the outlaws of Mount Liang, which were by now renowned throughout the Song Empire for their courage and willingness to speak out for justice and freedom.

Song led the outlaws in a ceremony to give thanks for heaven's blessings and to pray for 'King' Chao and all those who had died or been injured in the fight against the unjust imperial forces and their allies. The outlaws appealed to the gods for the opportunity to serve a righteous and fair government which truly looked after all the people.

Suddenly there was a bright flash in the sky above them and everyone looked up.

Boom!

There was a roar of thunder and a bolt of lightning, and a fireball streaked across the sky. With a mighty rush it hit the earth and disappeared. Chao sent out a party of outlaws to look for the place where the fireball had buried itself, and when they found the hole they discovered a stone tablet with ancient writings engraved into it.

A scholar was invited to decipher the writings. They turned out to be the names of the one hundred and eight commanders of the outlaws, each the reincarnation of one of the thirty-six heavenly spirits and seventy-two earthly demons released by the arrogant Marshall Hong so many years before.

'My dear brothers,' Song addressed the outlaws, 'As our names correspond with the heavenly spirits and earthly demons recorded

on this stone tablet, it appears to be the heaven's wish that we do everything we can to look after our country and people, just as the gods have always done. Let us not disappoint the gods.'

Although this is where our story of the Mount Liang outlaws ends, the world did not suddenly become a place without greed and injustice, corruption and the misuse of power. Wherever the laws are unjust, and the people are not free, there will always be a need for courageous outlaws willing to fight for fairness and justice.

TAKING THINGS FURTHER
The real read

The *Real Reads* version of *The Water Margin* is a retelling in English of Shi Nai'an's gripping (and very long!) Chinese work. If you would like to read the full Chinese version in all its original splendour, you will need to learn the Chinese language. Otherwise you will have to rely on one of the English translations whose details you will find on page 60.

Filling in the spaces

The loss of so many of Shi Nai'an's original words is a sad but necessary part of the shortening process. We have had to make some difficult decisions, omitting subplots and characters, some important, some less so, but all interesting. We have also, at times, taken the liberty of combining two events into one, or of giving a character words or actions that originally belong to another. The points below will fill in some of the gaps, but nothing can beat the original.

- Shi Nai'an gives a much more detailed description about Gao Qiu's background and rise to power than we have space for. There is also much more about the events in the lives of the book's one hundred and nine heroes (Chao Gai and the earthly manifestations of one hundred and eight spirits) that lead them to eventually become the 'righteous bandits' of Mount Liang.

- Shi devotes many pages of his book to describing the friendships formed, as well as the conflicts arising, among the heroes. There are also far more battles launched either by the government troops or by the outlaws throughout their attempts to take over districts, cities, towns and villages, involving the use of all sorts of deceptions, frauds, tricks, traps, and even magic.

- In Shi's *Water Margin* three of the outlaws are women. They are Hu Sanniang, a brilliant woman warrior whose marriage to one of the outlaws is arranged by Song Jiang; Sun Erniang, an innkeeper's wife who is notorious for making buns filled with human flesh; and Big Sister Gu, another female innkeeper who is determined to rescue her two innocent brothers from prison.

● In the full version Song Jiang repeatedly refuses to join the outlaws before he finally gives in and agrees to. Even after he joins them and eventually becomes their leader, he regularly suggests that the outlaws accept the government's offer of amnesty and become 'good citizens'.

● An important incident in Song's early life is that he has a dream in which a goddess presents him with three 'heavenly scrolls' that detail the art of war. It is with the help of the numerous strategies found in these scrolls that Song is able to lead the outlaws in their righteous fight against the government.

● Song keeps insisting that Lu Junyi should be made the leader of the outlaws. Although Song is eventually elected as the leader, it is Lu who foresees the end of the outlaws in a dream in which the outlaws decide to surrender to the government but are all executed as criminals.

Back in time

Shi Nai'an wrote *The Water Margin* in the fourteenth century. It is based on the exploits of the historical outlaw Song Jiang and his thirty-six companions during the Northern Song Dynasty (960–1127). The group was active in the marshlands surrounding Mount Liang in eastern China, attacking government troops and sustaining citizens in need. In Shi's book, the number of Song's outlaws has been expanded to one hundred and eight.

In his book, Shi successfully combines historical records with folk tales about the Mount Liang outlaws, and adds a flavour of myth and magic to their stories, describing them as earthly manifestations of thirty-six heavenly spirits and seventy-two earthly demons. This, together with Shi's rich and often humorous portrayal of the outlaws, has meant that *The Water Margin* has remained one of the most popular Chinese books ever written.

During the Yuan Dynasty, when Shi was writing *The Water Margin*, there was widespread resentment towards China's Mongol rulers, and *The Water Margin* with its themes of citizen revolt and popular uprising became a common source for dramatic adaptation. Stories of the Mount Liang outlaws reflected a desire among the common people to rise up against a cruel and unjust government. It is no wonder that later, during the Ming Dynasty when the government became increasingly corrupt and incompetent, the Emperor decided to ban Shi's book!

Despite its popularity, there is a traditional warning in Chinese that young people should not read *The Water Margin*, as the book places an unhealthy emphasis on violence, brawls and male machismo (the same warning goes on to say that old people should not read

The Three Kingdoms – also available in *Real Reads* – because it might give them dangerous ideas about fraud and deception). With the exception of the three women outlaws, the few female characters in the book are almost always depicted as being selfish and deserving to be punished. *The Water Margin* is often thought of as a 'bad boys' book' with some very questionable ideas about what 'brotherhood' really means.

Nonetheless, *The Water Margin* holds an important position in China's literary history as the first full-length work written in everyday Chinese as opposed to a high literary style. Its descriptions of ordinary people's lives, practices, views and beliefs are highly convincing, and have enriched numerous other forms of art. The codes of ethics highlighted in the book, such as responsibility, justice, friendship and family duty, have been important in developing Chinese thinking.

Finding out more

We recommend the following English books and websites to gain a greater understanding of Shi Nai'an and his writings:

Books

- Pearl S. Buck (trans.), *All Men are Brothers*, Moyer Bell, Tra edition, 2004. This is one of the earliest English translations of *The Water Margin* and was first published in 1933.

- Sidney Shapiro (trans.), *Outlaws of the Marsh*, Beijing Foreign Language Press, 1993. This is considered to be one of the best English translations of *The Water Margin* and was first published in 1980.

- J.H. Jackson (trans.), *The Water Margin: Outlaws of the Marsh*, Tuttle Publishing, 2010. This is a detailed translation more faithful to the Chinese version.

Websites

- www.poisonpie.com/words/others/somewhat/outlaws/index.html
'Outlaws of the Marsh: A Somewhat Less than Critical Commentary' by David Keffer, which introduces the history and English translations of *The Water Margin* as well as its prominent characters and quotes.

- http://aubord_de_l_eau.perso.sfr.fr/English/Romanx.html
A site that introduces, in English and French, the characters and episodes of *The Water Margin* and paper-cuts which represent them.

- http://history.cultural-china.com/en/171History5130.html
A site that contains twenty-one prominent characters of *The Water Margin* in paintings.

- http://en.wikipedia.org/wiki/Water_Margin
The Wikipedia page about *The Water Margin*, with links to other pages about the book's author and main characters.

- www.youtube.com/watch?v=Yy6qEUmbZ1Y
The theme song of *The Water Margin* as a television series, which was produced by the Japanese in 1973. This version, dubbed in English, was shown on BBC television between 1976 and 1978.

Food for thought

Here are some things to think about if you are reading *The Water Margin* alone, or ideas for discussion if you are reading it with friends.
In retelling *The Water Margin* we have tried to recreate, as accurately as possible, Shi Nai'an's original plot and characters. We have also tried to imitate aspects of his style. Remember, however, that this is not the original work; thinking about the points below, therefore, can help you begin to understand Shi's craft. To move forward from here, turn to the abridged or full-length English translations of *The Water Margin* and lose yourself in his wonderful storytelling.

Starting points

● Which character interests you the most? Why?

● Do you agree with the heroes in *The Water Margin* that being a 'righteous outlaw' is a good way to serve your country and people? Does your view change as you read on? How?

● Can you think of any individual or group of individuals throughout the history whose adventures were similar to those of the Mount Liang outlaws? Why do you think these stories are famous?

● If Shi Nai'an was writing today, do you think the heroes of his book would still be a group of outlaws?

Themes

What do you think Shi is saying about the following themes in *The Water Margin*?

● friendship

● loyalty

- compassion
- teamwork
- courage

Style

Can you find paragraphs in *The Water Margin* that contain examples of the following?

- descriptions of setting and atmosphere
- the use of a very simple sentence to achieve a particular effect
- a character exposing their true character through something they say or the way they behave
- humour

Look closely at how these paragraphs are written. What do you notice? Can you write a paragraph in the same style?